THE LOST AND FOUND HOUSE

by **Michael Cadnum**

paintings by **Steve Johnson** and **Lou Fancher**

VIKING

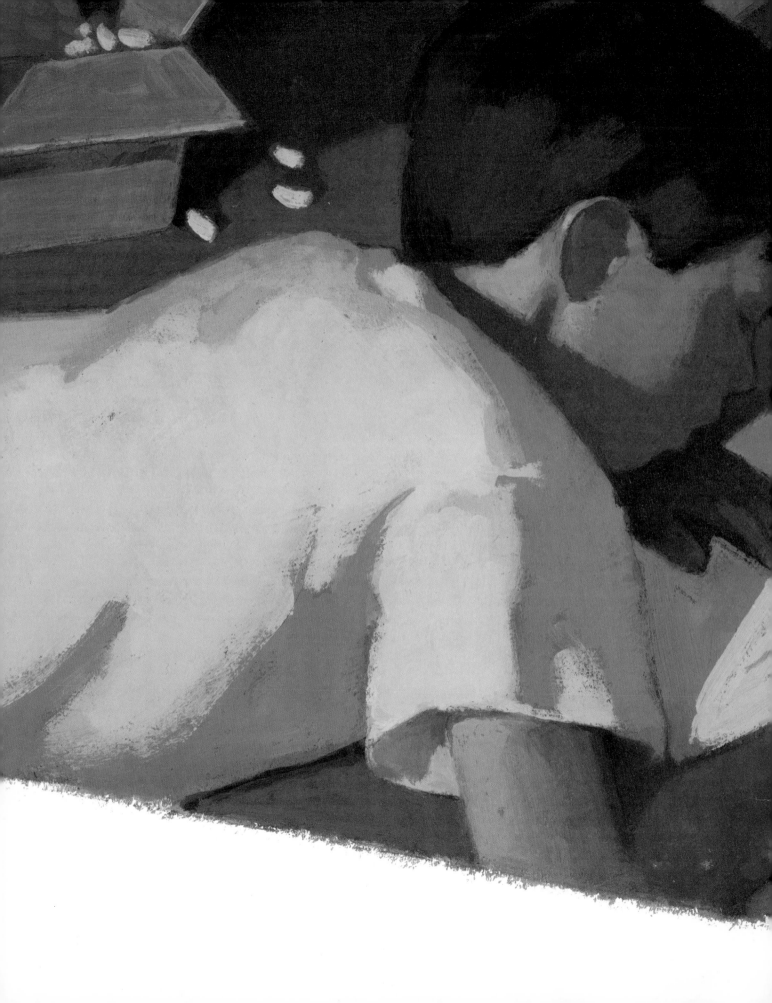

We all saw the new house,
in the new town far away, months ago,
but now I can hardly imagine it.
When I think of the new house,
it has no color and it keeps changing shape.

The moving men load the sofa and the rolled-up rugs
and the painting of the red horses.
They carry out the aquarium that used to hold fish.
They carry out the boxes taped shut.
Plates rattle in the plate box.

"Almost done," say the moving men.
As they close the door of the big blue van, they wave.
"Goodbye," they call, and Dad waves and Mom waves
and I do, too, but when I say goodbye,
I whisper.

Our house is empty.
Dad's steps echo, and Mom and I
check the empty rooms
to see the things which are not there.

Here is where the sofa sat,
and here is where the television plugged in,
and here is where the roller skates
tumbled downstairs all by themselves
and left a trail of dents in the steps.

"The traffic will be awful," says Dad,
but Mom says nothing at all.
Dad spends a long time
finding the right key for the car.
"I hope the traffic isn't too bad,"
says Mom at last, in a very quiet voice,
and Dad starts the car.
"Goodbye, old house," says Dad.

There goes the old gas station.
And there goes the old school.
And there goes the house
where the growling dog lived.
And there goes the hole
where the pepper tree blew down
and never grew back.

At night the headlights make the world look big.
We stay in a motel where the glasses are wrapped in plastic.
I bounce on my great big bed, and no one tells me to stop.
"Tomorrow is a big day," says Dad.

We sleep in the motel room.
All night trucks rumble past.
But I hardly really sleep.

In the morning I have a scrambled egg mixed with cheese,
and toast with warm, soggy butter, and I even eat the parsley.
Dad eats his, too. "If that's the thing to do,"
he says, winking at me.
Mom doesn't even eat her toast.

The new town has tall, straight trees.
It has a stadium and a big empty parking lot.
It has gulls and a bay and ships.

None of us talk except Dad.
"There's the new grocery store," he says,
"and there's the new drugstore, and there's the new school."

The school has more tall, straight trees and a long, green field.
Children kick a soccer ball, and a white gull
glides down to the middle of the basketball court.

"Here's our street," says Dad.
A striped cat watches a
black-and-white dog trot down the sidewalk,
followed by two children on bicycles.

The moving men are there already,
lifting furniture wrapped in gray blankets
out of the blue van.

At last the new house is full of boxes and furniture,
and the aquarium that used to have fish.

Outside, the garden is all weeds,
and a red rubber ball so old it is gray
hides under a bush with red berries.

There is a rusty bucket full of white flowers,
and a faucet that won't turn on
no matter how hard I try.

An orange Frisbee sails up and falls at my feet.
I throw it back, and there are children at the top of the fence.

They say who they are: a boy named Terence
and his sister named Nicole.

All night I keep waking, and think:
I know where I am.
Because each time, I have forgotten.

In the morning the light is yellow under the door, and I open it.

The windows have no curtains, so the sun is all over the hall.

Sun is all over the kitchen, and Mom and Dad
are holding up the picture of the red horses and saying
it can't go here and it can't go there.

When I stand on the front steps,
the orange Frisbee rolls across the lawn.
The air smells like ocean.
The black-and-white dog is waiting
with Nicole and Terence.

The Frisbee has stopped rolling. The grass squeaks under my feet.

And when I throw the Frisbee back, it stops in midair,
and doesn't go forward and doesn't fall.

Until Terence lifts his hand and takes it
from the air, turns, and throws it back again.
I catch it, with one hand.

That night Mom is singing softly to herself,
putting up bookshelves. And I know that
one morning the aquarium will bubble quietly,

and swimming through the green plants
and the ceramic castle and the miniature bridge,
there will be fish.

For Adam and Jessica
—M. C.

For Don, our #1 mover, and Dale/Zeus
—S. J. & L. F.

VIKING
Published by the Penguin Group
Penguin Putnam Inc., 375 Hudson Street, New York, New York 10014, U.S.A.
Penguin Books Ltd, 27 Wrights Lane, London W8 5TZ, England
Penguin Books Australia Ltd, Ringwood, Victoria, Australia
Penguin Books Canada Ltd, 10 Alcorn Avenue, Toronto, Ontario, Canada M4V 3B2
Penguin Books (N.Z.) Ltd, 182-190 Wairau Road, Auckland 10, New Zealand

Penguin Books Ltd, Registered Offices: Harmondsworth, Middlesex, England

First published in 1997 by Viking, a member of Penguin Putnam Inc.

1 3 5 7 9 10 8 6 4 2

Text copyright © Michael Cadnum, 1997
Illustrations copyright © Steve Johnson and Lou Fancher, 1997
All rights reserved

LIBRARY OF CONGRESS CATALOGING-IN-PUBLICATION DATA
Cadnum, Michael.
The lost and found house / by Michael Cadnum ; illustrated by Steve Johnson and Lou Fancher.
p. cm.
Summary: A young boy describes how he and his parents feel when
they leave their old house and move to a new house in another town.
ISBN 0-670-84884-0
[1. Moving, Household—Fiction.] I. Johnson, Steve, ill.
II. Fancher, Lou, ill. III. Title.
PZ7.C11724Lo 1997 [E]—dc21 96-37256 CIP AC

Designed by Lou Fancher
Printed in U.S.A.
Set in Stone Serif